HOLLY

The true story of a cat

for James and Helen

A Red Fox Book

Published by Random House Children's Books
20 Vauxhall Bridge Road, London SW1V 2SA

A division of The Random House Group Ltd
London Melbourne Sydney Auckland
Johannesburg and agencies throughout the world

Copyright © Ruth Brown 1999
Copyright endpapers © James Brown 1999

1 3 5 7 9 10 8 6 4 2

First published in Great Britain by The Andersen Press Ltd. 1999

Red Fox edition 2001

Printed in Hong Kong by Midas Printing Limited

THE RANDOM HOUSE GROUP Limited Reg. No. 954009

www.randomhouse.co.uk

ISBN 0 09 941345 0

HOLLY

The true story of a cat

Ruth Brown

RED FOX

Dear Reader,

Fourteen years ago, on a cold November day, someone found a tiny, abandoned kitten. By coincidence they took her to our local vet, who knew that we wanted a kitten. Our dear old cat, Flossie, had died and the house seemed very empty without her. So we were delighted to welcome this small, homeless creature into our lives.

She was scraggy and thin and very nervous, but gradually she got used to us and settled into her new home. As she became more confident, she spent long, happy days investigating and exploring her exciting new world. But sometimes she would sit quite still, thinking deep thoughts.

When she was completely grown, she had two kittens of her own – a big boy and a tiny girl. We called them Buddy and Baby. She looked after them really well when they were little, but when they too were grown up she got rather bored with them. She always tried to sneak off on her own for some peace and quiet, but the other two usually found her.

She is an old lady now but she is still the boss. She is also still quick enough to catch me "presents". In fact, she brought me one this morning – I think she knew it was my birthday. Often she turns her back on the world and ignores everybody. Yet, every afternoon when I am working, she still comes and sits on my desk and keeps me company for a while.

So, this book is about her, and how she grew from being a tiny, frightened kitten into our big, beautiful and beloved Holly.

Ruth Brown
20th May, 1999

She was just a tiny kitten and she was abandoned.

Someone found her

and gave her to us.

Because it was nearly Christmas

we called her Holly.

She was timid Holly, at first...

but as she grew she became relaxed Holly

inquisitive Holly

acrobatic Holly

adventurous Holly

fearless Holly

intelligent Holly

silly Holly

proud Holly

bored Holly

nosy Holly

exhausted Holly

bossy Holly

generous Holly

grumpy Holly

affectionate Holly

big, beautiful,

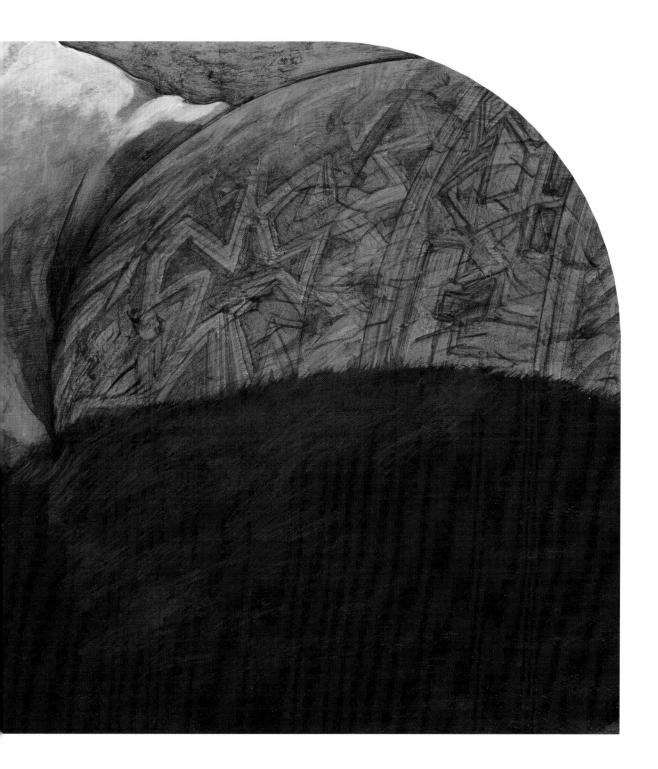

beloved Holly.

More Red Fox picture books
for you to enjoy

MUMMY LAID AN EGG
by Babette Cole 0099299119

RUNAWAY TRAIN
by Benedict Blathwayt 0099385716

DOGGER
by Shirley Hughes 009992790X

WHERE THE WILD THINGS ARE
by Maurice Sendak 0099408392

OLD BEAR
by Jane Hissey 0099265761

MISTER MAGNOLIA
by Quentin Blake 0099400421

ALFIE GETS IN FIRST
by Shirley Hughes 0099855607

OI! GET OFF OUR TRAIN
by John Burningham 009985340X

GORGEOUS
by Caroline Castle and Sam Childs 0099400766